MW01140086

DISCARD

WELCOME TO MEXICO WITH SESAME STREET

CHRISTY PETERSON

Lerner Publications ◆ Minneapolis

In this series, *Sesame Street* characters help readers learn about other countries' people, cultures, landscapes, and more. These books connect friends around the world while giving readers new tools to become smarter, kinder friends. Pack your bags and take a fun-filled look at your world with your funny, furry friends from *Sesame Street*.

—Sincerely, the Editors at Sesame Street

TABLE OF CONTENTS

WELCOME TO MEXICO!

¡Hola, amigo! My name is Lola. *Yaní*, *xamigua*, and *nahí* are all ways to say *friend* in Mexico!

4

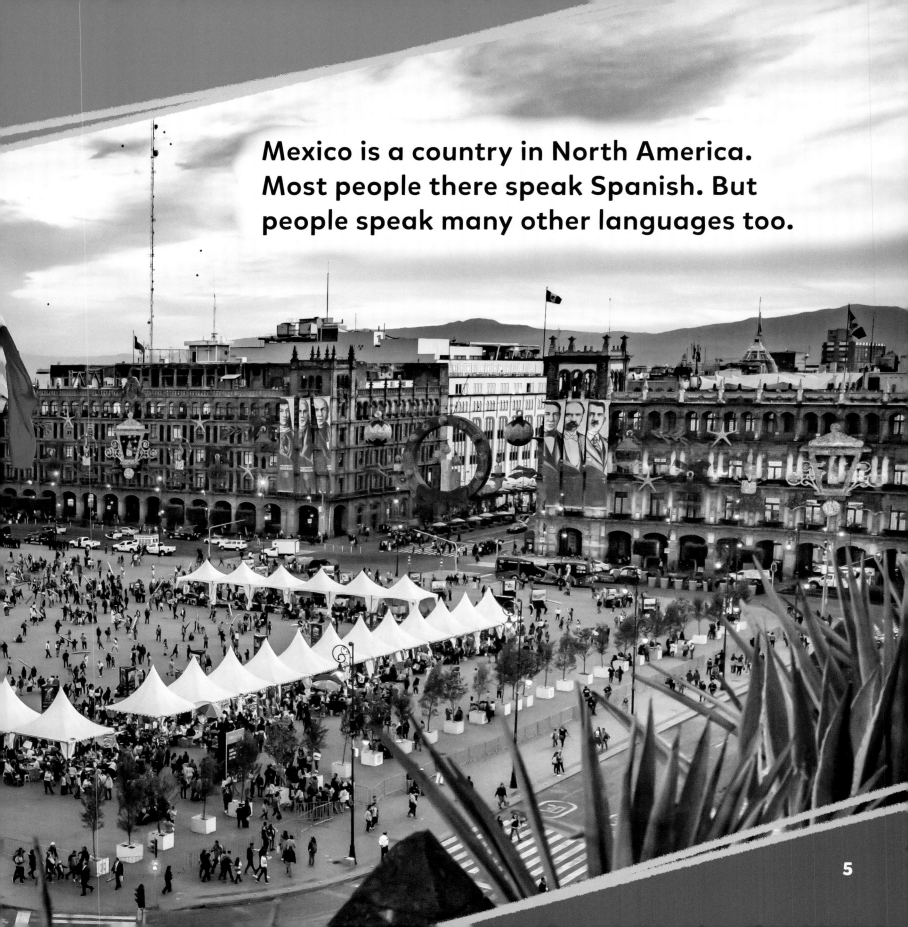

Mexico is a country in North America. Most people there speak Spanish. But people speak many other languages too.

WHERE IN THE WORLD IS MEXICO?

Mexico and Surrounding Area

California
Arizona
New Mexico
UNITED STATES
Texas
N

Miles
0   100   200   300
0   200   400
Kilometers

Gulf of Mexico

MEXICO

PACIFIC OCEAN

Mexico City ★

BELIZE

GUATEMALA

NORTH AMERICA

Mexico

ATLANTIC OCEAN

PACIFIC OCEAN

SOUTH AMERICA

ARCTIC OCEAN

ASIA

EUROPE

AFRICA

PACIFIC
OCEAN

INDIAN
OCEAN

AUSTRALIA

SOUTHERN OCEAN

Mexico has many kinds of land. There are deserts, rain forests, beaches, and mountains.

Most of northern Mexico is desert like this.

9

People lived in Mexico hundreds of years ago.
You can still visit some of the pyramids they built.

Today, most people live in cities.

In Mexico City, you can visit gardens surrounded by water.

The gardens are called chinampas (chee-nahm-pahs). You take a boat called a *trajinera* (tra-hee-neh-ra) to see them.

Relationships with family members are very important. In Mexico, families like to spend a lot of time together!

15

Día de Muertos means "Day of the Dead." On this holiday, families remember loved ones who have died.

Día de Muertos is a happy time. People share special food and light candles.

17

Tortillas are a common food in Mexico. Corn, beans, and peppers are also important foods.

19

Mariachi play music on guitars, trumpets, and other instruments. People in Mexico love music, just like you!

¡Adiós, amigos! That means "goodbye, friends" in Spanish!

20

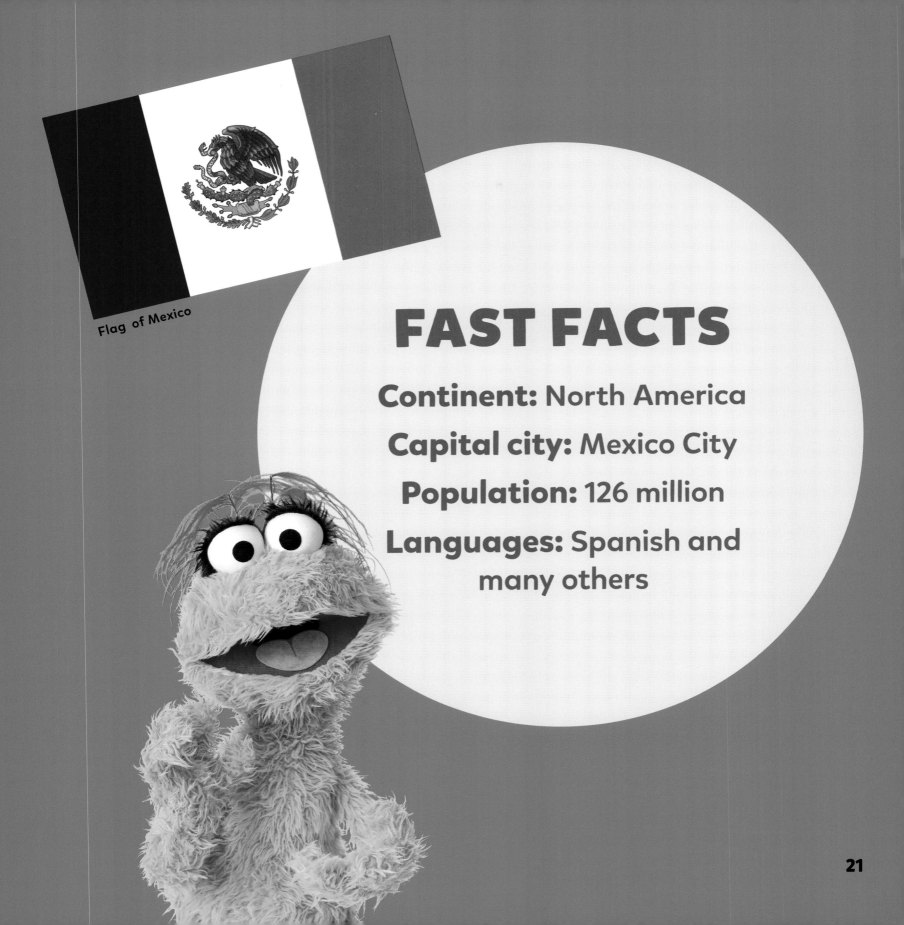

Flag of Mexico

FAST FACTS

Continent: North America

Capital city: Mexico City

Population: 126 million

Languages: Spanish and many others

GLOSSARY

amigo: the Spanish word for "friend"

chinampa: a traditional garden in Mexico grown on raised mounds of dirt and surrounded by water

mariachi: a small band of musicians that play mostly string instruments

pyramid: a building with a square base and four triangular sides that meet in a point

rain forest: a forest that gets lots of rain all year

relationship: a connection between people

trajinera: a boat with a flat bottom

LEARN MORE

Eliot, Hannah. *Día de los Muertos*. New York: Little Simon, 2018.

Moon, Walt K. *Let's Explore Mexico*. Minneapolis: Lerner Publications, 2017.

Pérez, Ma. Alma González. *¡Todos a Comer! A Mexican Food Alphabet Book*. Zapata, TX: Del Alma, 2017.

INDEX

Photo Acknowledgments

Additional Image credits: bpperry/Getty Images, pp. 4–5; Laura Westlund/Independent Picture Service, pp. 6–7, 21; ©fitopardo/Getty Images, p. 8; Ondrej Prosicky/Shutterstock.com, p. 9; javarman/Shutterstock.com, p. 10; K_Boonnitrod/Shutterstock.com, p. 11; archishooting/Shutterstock.com, p. 12; Claudio Briones/Shutterstock.com, p. 13; aldomurillo/Getty Images, p. 14; Mick Ritzel/Alamy Stock Photo, p. 15; phortun/Shutterstock.com, p. 16; Alejandro_Munoz/Shutterstock.com, p. 17; Marcos Castillo/Shutterstock.com, p. 18; Lorenza Ochoa/Shutterstock.com, p. 20.

Cover: posztos/Shutterstock.com (top); Lorena Huerta/Shutterstock.com (bottom).

Lerner Publications Company
An imprint of Lerner Publishing Group, Inc.
241 First Avenue North
Minneapolis, MN 55401 USA

For reading levels and more information, look up this title at www.lernerbooks.com.

Main body text set in Mikado a Regular.
Typeface provided by HVD Fonts.

Photo Editor: Brianna Kaiser

Library of Congress Cataloging-in-Publication Data

Names: Peterson, Christy, author.
Title: Welcome to Mexico with Sesame Street / Christy Peterson.
Description: Minneapolis : Lerner Publications, 2022. | Series: Sesame Street friends around the world | Includes bibliographical references and index. | Audience: Ages 4–8 | Audience: Grades K–1 | Summary: "Readers discover the big cities, tropical rain forests, and colorful celebrations of Mexico alongside their Sesame Street pals. Learn about popular foods such as beans and tortillas, how Mexican families honor their ancestors, and more"—Provided by publisher.
Identifiers: LCCN 2020044752 (print) | LCCN 2020044753 (ebook) | ISBN 9781728424361 (library binding) | ISBN 9781728431550 (paperback) | ISBN 9781728430461 (ebook)
Subjects: LCSH: Mexico—Juvenile literature. | Mexico—Social life and customs—Juvenile literature.
Classification: LCC F1208.5 .P48 2022 (print) | LCC F1208.5 (ebook) | DDC 972—dc23

LC record available at https://lccn.loc.gov/2020044752
LC ebook record available at https://lccn.loc.gov/2020044753

Manufactured in the United States of America
1-49306-49422-2/17/2021